Quiz No 219586
Robot Goalie

Hurn, Roge
B.L.2.7
Points: 0.5

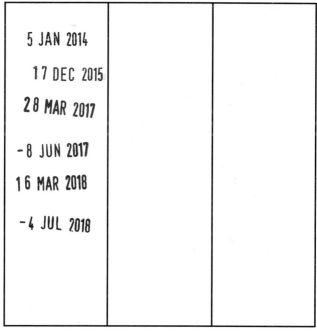

BEDALE HIGH SCHOOL LRC

This item is to be returned on or before the last date stamped below

5 JAN 2014		
17 DEC 2015		
28 MAR 2017		
-8 JUN 2017		
16 MAR 2018		
-4 JUL 2018		

Fines are 2p per day up to a maximum of 50p per item

2013

14258

Titles in More First Flight

Comic Chaos	Jonny Zucker
Into The Deep	Jonny Zucker
Cyber Phone	Richard Taylor
Mutt	Jane A C West
Captured!	Alison Hawes
Robot Goalie	Roger Hurn
Alien Eggs	Danny Pearson
Just in Time	Jane A C West
The Speed Flyers	Jonny Zucker
Super Teacher	Stan Cullimore

Badger Publishing Limited
Suite G08, Business & Technology Centre
Bessemer Drive, Stevenage, Hertfordshire SG1 2DX
Telephone: 01438 791037   Fax: 01438 791036
www.badger-publishing.co.uk

Robot Goalie ISBN 978-1-84926-456-3

Badger Publishing would like to thank Jonny Zucker for his help
in putting this series together.

Publisher: David Jamieson
Senior Editor: Danny Pearson
Design: Fiona Grant
Illustration: Mark Penman

CONTENTS

CHAPTER 1	**The Attic**	PAGE 5
CHAPTER 2	**The Plan**	PAGE 10
CHAPTER 3	**The Competition**	PAGE 13
CHAPTER 4	**No Goalie!**	PAGE 16
CHAPTER 5	**The Shoot Out**	PAGE 22
INVENTORS AND INVENTIONS		PAGE 30
QUESTIONS		PAGE 32

New words:

code	puzzled
flyer	goalie
inventor	awesome
striker	competition

Main characters:

Finn

Eve

The robot

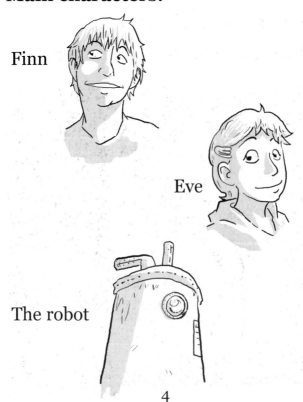

CHAPTER 1
The Attic

It is the summer holidays. Eve and Finn are staying with their Nan.

She lives in a big old house.
It is raining. Eve and Finn are bored.

They go up to the attic. It is dusty and full of junk. They find a big brown envelope in a box.

The words "My Last Invention" are written on it. "Let's show this to Nan," says Eve.

Nan is in the kitchen.

"Look at this," says Finn.

Nan smiles. "That is your Great Uncle Harry's writing," she says.

Eve and Finn are puzzled. "Who is Great Uncle Harry?" asks Eve.

"Harry was a nutty inventor," says Nan.

"He was always thinking up crazy inventions."

"Hey, that's cool," says Finn.

"I wonder what his last invention is?" says Eve.

"Open the envelope and find out," says Nan.

CHAPTER 2

The Plan

Eve and Finn open the envelope.
Inside is a plan of an odd looking
machine.

"I can't read the words on the plan,"
says Finn. "They are not English
words."

Nan looks at them. "They are written in Harry's secret code," she says. "No one can read it. He didn't want anyone to steal his ideas."

Finn and Eve look hard at the words on the plan.

"I think I can break the code," says Eve.

"How?" asks Finn.

Eve says the letters in the words are written back to front.

She writes them the right way round.

"Look," she says, "EHT TOBOR EILAOG is really THE ROBOT GOALIE."

"Wow, you're smart," says Finn. "Now we can make it."

Nan shakes her head. "Don't waste your time," she says. "None of Harry's inventions ever worked."

CHAPTER 3
The Competition

A flyer comes through the letterbox.

It says the local football team is having an open day. There will be lots of competitions.

The big one is a penalty shoot out for goalies. The goalies must stop Sevano, the team's star striker scoring.

The prize is a pair of VIP tickets to the first game of the season.

"Let's make the robot goalie," says Finn. "I bet it will save all Sevano's shots."

"Great idea," says Eve. "But we can't do it."

Finn frowns. "Why not? We can read the plan."

"Yes, but we don't have all the things we need to build the robot."

Finn looks cross.

"Oh yes, you do," says Nan. "Harry left all his tools and things in my garage. You can use those."

Eve and Finn jump up and down.

"Hurray!" yells Finn. "Come on, Eve. We've got work to do!"

CHAPTER 4

No Goalie!

Eve and Finn make the robot goalie.

They take it to the local park to try it out.

They put it between some goal posts.

It looks weird.

Two boys make fun of it. "Your robot couldn't catch a cold," they say.
"It's got no chance of stopping Sevano's shots."

Finn and Eve take turns to kick a ball
at the robot goalie.

The robot saves every shot.

The two boys stop laughing.

"That robot is good," says one boy.

"It's not good - it's awesome," says the other boy.

"Yes," says Finn. "It's going to win the competition."

"And we'll get the two VIP tickets for the next big match," says Eve.

The two boys follow Finn and Eve home.

They see Finn and Eve put the robot goalie in Nan's garage.

They grin at each other.

They make a plan to come back and steal it. They are going to pretend they made it. They want to win the competition.

The next morning, Finn and Eve go to the garage. They see the door is open.

The robot has gone!

"Oh no," says Finn. "Someone has stolen our robot goalie!"

"Yes," says Eve, "and it's too late to make another one. The competition is today."

CHAPTER 5

The Shoot Out

Eve and Finn go to the stadium anyway.

They see their robot goalie. It is with the two boys.

"Hey, that's our robot," says Finn. "You stole it."

"Yes," says Eve. "Now give it back."

The boys laugh at them. "You can't prove that," they say. "It is ours now."

The shoot out starts.

Sevano scores against all the goalies.

Now it is turn of the robot goalie.

It saves all his shots.

The club coach, Terry Johnson says, "You boys win the prize. Here are your VIP tickets".

The boys go to take the tickets. But the robot goalie starts kicking footballs at Sevano.

"Stop that robot," shouts Terry, "It's going to hurt my star striker."

The two boys don't know how to stop it. "We didn't make the robot," they say.

"They did." The two boys point at Finn and Eve. Then they run away.

Terry looks at Finn and Eve. "Quick! Do something!" he says.

Eve pulls out the plans.

She reads them. "Got it!" she shouts.
"The lever at the back of the robot will
stop it."

Finn dashes up to the robot goalie.

He pulls the lever.

The robot stops kicking balls at Sevano.

"Well done," says Terry. "The top prize is yours."

Finn and Eve take the robot goalie home.

They show Nan their VIP tickets.

"Great Uncle Harry would be so proud," says Nan. "At last one of his inventions really worked!"

INVENTORS AND INVENTIONS

- *Leonardo Da Vinci was a great inventor.*

- *He used mirror writing when he wrote down his ideas.*

- *He did this by writing backwards. You can only read mirror writing by holding it up to a mirror.*

- *Leonardo lived hundreds of years ago but he designed a tank, a helicopter and a parachute.*

- *Leonardo was a genius.*

FINN AND EVE'S INVENTOR JOKE

- *Eve: Did you hear about the inventor who invented a gas that can burn through anything?*

- *Finn: Yes, now he's trying to invent something to keep it in!*

QUESTIONS

- What do Eve and Finn find in Nan's attic?

- What does Great Uncle Harry do?

- Why can't Finn read Great Uncle Harry's writing?

- What is the prize in the competition?

- What is the name of the star striker?

- How does Finn stop the robot goalie?

- Why does Nan say that Great Uncle Harry would be so proud?